Shhh!
A Flash Fiction Library

Shhh!
A Flash Fiction Library

Matthew Roy Davey

Chapeltown Books

British Library Cataloguing in Publication Data

A Record of this Publication is available from the British Library

ISBN 978-1-915762-29-0

This edition published 2025 by Chapeltown Books
Manchester, England

Contents

Introduction

This collection of flash fiction is not designed to be read from cover to cover, though you may, of course, read it that way if you wish. The volume has been organised, for your convenience, into sections like those in a library. The Dewey Decimal system has not been employed. Simply browse the shelves until you find something in a section that appeals to you. Each "bite-sized" story can thus be consumed in the time that it takes you to, for example: smoke a cigarette or wait in a car while a friend or relative is shopping. For convenience, why not keep a copy in your bathroom or the glove compartment of your vehicle?

You will notice that next to each title is a box for you to tick so you know which ones have been read, or "taken out". Just make sure you use a pencil (not included) so the ticks can be erased when you send the book to a charity shop. You may find some stories do not fit particularly well in their designated section of the library. You may even feel they have been "miss-filed". This will particularly be the case in the so-called "Romance" section. Don't blame me, this happens in real libraries, where they still exist. Some sections are also better represented than others. For example, "Crime" and "Children" have plenty of entries while "Sport" has only one. This is because Crime and Children are far more interesting than Sport. You will notice that there is no "Humour" section. Don't say you weren't warned.

ANIMALS

Mousetrap

At first it was movements in the corner of the eye, so fast, so sudden that we weren't sure we'd seen anything. There were no droppings, no chewed boxes; it wasn't until I came down the stairs one evening and saw him running around the hallway that I was sure. He stopped and sat on his haunches, looking up at me as he washed his whiskers, paws curling over his nose, a bold little fellow. It was almost insolent.

The next morning, I bought four mousetraps of the old-fashioned spring-loaded variety, and baited them with peanut butter. It was what mice liked best I'd read. Some websites claimed that mice preferred Cadbury's Fruit and Nut, but that was my favourite and I was damned if I'd share with an uninvited rodent. Besides, I felt the stickiness of peanut butter might prove more adhesive and effective and so I loaded the traps and placed them in strategic locations.

It took around forty-eight hours for the first to be sprung, the one under the cooker. I was in at the time, working at the computer. The snap seemed to echo around the house. My stomach went cold but at the same time I felt a buzz of satisfaction. I picked up the adjustable spanner I'd put ready and made my way to the kitchen. My steps felt heavy, each one bringing me closer to something awful.

The mouse was still moving, trying to pull free of the trap which had shut on its nose. When it saw me coming it began to scream, high and desperate, louder than I'd have thought possible. As I got closer, I saw its front paws had been severed by the trap. Its back legs scrabbled on the lino as it tried to escape, desperate to stay alive. After a moment's hesitation I hit it with the spanner, square on the head, and the squeaking stopped. It should have been over, but the back end began dancing, jerking in a spastic frenzy. I hit it again and again, pulverising the little body. Eventually the mouse lay still, and I sat breathing hard and feeling dreadful, watching the redness spread across the floor, amazed there could be so much blood in such a small creature. I felt like a man and didn't want to be one.

Elsie's Dog

There were raised eyebrows when Elsie bought Carlos. Did she really have the energy for a puppy at her age?

When Elsie had a stroke, her sons resisted the urge to say "told you so," but also resisted her pleas to take Carlos.

A solution was found; a son's friend agreed to have Carlos. He sent photographs of the dog to Elsie in the old folk's home. His kids loved Carlos. The pictures brought Elsie great peace of mind.

~~Carlos was also pleased.~~

He hated Elsie.

She smelled of death.

Bulldog

It was a bright evening in early spring, and I was walking through the gates of Eastville Park by The Queens Head. A squirrel darted past my leg and cut across in front of me, flashing back towards the park and up the boundary wall. I heard a shout, high and female, and then the scrabble of claws as a bulldog barrelled past, shoving my leg to get by. Unaware of the squirrel's change in trajectory, it thundered across the pavement, lumbering into the rush-hour traffic on Fishponds Road, into the path of a speeding white van.

The voice screamed again, and I heard something fall, contents rattling, scattering, her footsteps slapping the tarmac. The dog stopped in the road, looked left and then, wham, it was gone. The van didn't brake or swerve, just sped on as though nothing had happened. The dog reappeared under the van's rear bumper, some strange physics spitting it high into the air where it flipped, spinning in a howling arc of piss that fountained in the evening air. It landed with a thud, in front of a Ford Mondeo that screeched to a halt.

The dog lay motionless.

Something rolled past my foot, a pound coin, and wobbled to a halt at the curb's edge. The woman raced past me, heading for the dog. The coin fell.

The dog clambered slowly to its feet and stood, legs braced, shaking its head with a jowly grunt.

I picked up the coin.

The woman attempted to gather the beast in her arms, but it howled as she tried to lift it, a screech of agony. She eased it onto the pavement where it lay, chest swelling and collapsing, swelling and collapsing.

I rolled the coin between finger and thumb, watching as a couple of bystanders crossed to the woman. Another woman had picked up the handbag and replaced the contents. She laid it at the woman's side, placing a hand on her shoulder for a moment.

I wasn't sure what to do. I couldn't pocket the money, but it didn't seem right to give it back at that moment. I looked around, wondering if anyone had seen me pick it up. People were offering the woman advice as she crouched, weeping over the dog. A man was standing a little way from the group, talking into his phone, a finger jammed in his unused ear. The traffic kept moving, people watching the drama as they passed, faces expressionless.

I walked across and edged sideways through the crowd, extending my arm, the coin held between finger and thumb, almost under her nose. She looked up and her mascara blurred eyes met mine.

"Your pound." I shrugged, making an apologetic face.

She didn't respond for a moment, just stared. When she spoke, it was as though to a child.

"Please… just… go away," she said.

I opened my mouth to speak, nodded and then ducked out of the cluster, slipping the coin into my pocket as I walked away.

Crow

God knows what had happened before I got there, but I found it lying on its back in the middle of the track. A wing flexed from the concrete as it turned its head, beak gaping. I freewheeled past, wondering if I should do something. As I dithered, distance passed along with responsibility. I could not be bothered to stop and turn, ride back up the hill, all for the miserable task of delivering mercy. As I peddled on, it suffered still, agonised and fearful. And I had made it so.

Summoning the Toads

The Mooney woman taught him how to do it. She was forbidden to be on the premises, but she called Alfie over one day when he was playing near the fence that bordered the lane. The call was a high fluttering whistle, dancing like a mountain stream. He had been building a den from old branches and bracken when he heard.

Alfie knew that if his parents found out he'd been talking to her he'd be given a "bloody good hiding", but his father was at work and his mother was in the living room drinking gin with her friends. His mother wouldn't pay him any mind until he was called in to dinner when his father came home.

Mrs Mooney's eyes sparkled through the hedgerow, green and gold, like cat's eyes. Alfie hadn't seen her since the day his father yelled at her, thrashing her yelping terrier with his stick. Alfie had no idea what caused the uproar, though there were mutterings later about dog dirt in the rose beds. Things had been cordial up until then. Mrs Mooney used to do the gardening and from what Alfie could gather, did a good job, but even then, his parents told him to keep away from her. She used to leave him little presents on the porch: bird's eggs, peculiar shaped stones or bits of wood, once a carving of a little man. If his parents found the gifts before Alfie got to them, they hurled them into the bushes, so he was always on the lookout when Mrs Mooney left for the day. She'd always give him a wave and a wink as she departed, the little terrier in tow, and if his parents weren't there he'd wave back.

Mr Mooney's eyes were unblinking through the foliage. There was a rustle and Alfie felt a tug. He looked down and saw a scrawny brown hand with a fistful of his jumper.

"Would you like to learn a trick my boy?" she whispered through the hedge. He nodded, smiling, her eyes drawing him in, glittering, unblinking.

"There is a toad," she said, "who lives under your house. I shall teach you to call him. There is a noise you can make." She paused a moment as though gathering her energies. "A secret noise. It is passed from mother to daughter, father to son, but I have no daughter, I have no son, so you, my lad, will have to do."

When she started to chuckle, he found himself laughing too.

That night he stood on the porch and made the sound as she had taught him. Nothing happened and he wondered if he'd got it wrong, wondered if she'd been teasing him, but she'd told him to persevere, that it may take time before the magic began to work, and so he kept trying.

Sure enough, on the fourth night, as he stood there intoning, he heard a flopping noise at his feet. He looked down. Staring up, blank and unblinking, eyes glowing an orangey red, was the toad who lived under the house. Its body pulsed as it breathed, the lumps and lines that ran down its body swelling and contracting. Alfie stared at it, fascinated and repulsed. The toad stared back.

Each night Alfie performed the ritual and each night the toad returned, growing familiar. Alfie named it after his headmaster, Jones, and caught worms to feed to his visitor. Twelve days after its first appearance, Jones failed to respond to the summons. Disappointed, worried that perhaps something had happened to the toad, Alfie went up to bed.

As he was brushing his teeth he heard his mother's voice, high and alarmed, calling from the porch. He heard his father's footsteps moving through the house, the sound of him opening the back door and then, after a moment's silence, Alfie heard his father use a word he had never heard him use before. A bad word.

Alfie rinsed his mouth and went into his parents' bedroom and over to the window. There in the darkness, motionless and unblinking on the lawn, were hundreds, maybe thousands of burning red eyes, all of them staring with blank and malevolent intent.

Alfie heard a low chuckle from the lane, and without knowing why, he found himself laughing.

Downstairs, his mother began to cry.

ARTS

Braz

As I made my way down the stairs I passed a pale young man, a gore soaked towel held to his head. The bouncer supporting him said I couldn't go in. The cistern over the urinals was smashed and chunks of porcelain lay on the black and white tiles. The floor was awash with blood, scintillating, bright, so bright. Three colours: red, white and black, perfect like a composition, truly beautiful, almost like life.

There was breath on my neck, hot and quick.

I joined the queue for the ladies, the line twittering with delight, not minding the wait.

The Prick

Jerry had a picture hanging on the wall of his study. He'd painted it himself; a view of Helvellyn. One of the best things he'd ever done. His fifteen-year-old son, Eddie, had scrawled a prick on it in red permanent marker. Jerry had only just finished it and the paint was barely dry. He didn't speak to Eddie for three days. The prick hung in the sky like a crude zeppelin. Eddie had known how much it meant to his father; that was why he'd drawn the prick.

Jerry had the painting framed behind glass, prick and all, and hung it on the landing. His wife hadn't approved, felt that he was trying to shame their son, so he moved it to the study. Jerry started taking friends upstairs to show them. Part of him thought it made the picture more "artistic", having the prick floating above the mountain in a clearly different media. Slightly Chapman brothers. He judged people on their reaction to the prick. Some laughed, some were shocked, some stifled laughter. Most were indifferent.

He and Eddie never spoke of it. They didn't really speak much at all.

BIOGRAPHY

The Quarry

I hadn't seen much of Neil for several years. At the end of primary school, he'd gone private and I'd gone comprehensive. I didn't think of him often, but a time came when my school friends were being dicks, not bullying exactly, but making sure I felt shit at least once a day: digs about my clothes, my ears, even my family. I'd become the focus for the group's malice and it was getting me down, the constant drips of disparagement. I found myself thinking of Neil; he may have had his faults, but he was never cruel. I gave him a call and we arranged to go for a bike ride.

It was good to see him again even though we'd both changed; he'd become more straight-laced, while I liked to think I'd turned into something of a bad boy. I enjoyed his shock when I pulled out a packet of cigarettes. We'd stopped by a railway. It was a warm day and we'd eaten our sandwiches, chatting as though no time had passed.

As we cycled back, I felt happy, like something had been fixed. The fact I felt so lonely at school didn't seem to matter anymore, my relationship with Neil would endure.

We stopped at Tytherington Quarry, leaning our bikes on the wall and gazing across the expanse of absent land, a vast play-pit of excavations, the creamy rock layered in lines and right angles. Blue water filled the bottom and here and there were huge vehicles made tiny by distance, all static.

Cars had been passing frequently so we didn't pay much attention when a yellow Ford Capri crunched to a halt and reversed to where we were standing.

As soon as the man got out of the passenger door, I knew we were in trouble. He was rangy, rat-like, with greased back hair and a moustache. The engine kept running but the driver and the woman in the back were watching and laughing.

"Hello boys," the man leered.

"Hello," we both replied.

"What are you up to then? Up to no good?"

"No." We spoke in unison, our voices small and I felt a surge of impotent rage and shame.

The man was enjoying himself. He glanced back at the car and laughed. I stared at the woman in the back. It seemed obscene that she should be laughing. Women weren't like that, were they? I expected it of men, but women? She stopped laughing and gave me the finger.

"You staring at my bird?"

I shook my head.

"You fancy her?"

In my peripheral vision I could see Neil shuffling, twitching. I wondered if he was getting an asthma attack.

The man jabbed a finger in my chest and I staggered back a step, the point of impact burning. I could smell him, the tart bite of sweat, cheap aftershave, cigarettes and beer.

"You want to fuck her?"

I could feel my face flushing at the word, at the idea.

"No."

"No? What's wrong with her? You saying my bird's ugly?"

Laughter from the car.

"No."

"That all you can say? 'No'?"

"No."

More laughter. The man looked back at his friends.

"Can you believe this little prick?" They laughed harder.

Neil was making himself as small as possible, eyes down, head down, drawing in all that could be noticed, relieved, it seemed, that I was the focus of torment. Rage curdled within me at his weakness, his refusal to help, that he was leaving it all to me.

"I want you to apologise," smiled the man.

"What for?"

"What *for?*" He cuffed me round the head. Not hard but a ring caught me and my hand went up to rub it before I could stop myself. More laughter. My face burned in humiliation. "What for? For calling my bird a dog."

"I didn't."

"You fucking did." Another cuff round the head.

Why was it just me? Why didn't he turn on Neil? I couldn't understand what I'd done, what it was about me.

"At least the little prick's learnt to say something else." He drew himself up, hands on his hips. "If you don't apologise…" he paused, glancing skyward, then looked back at me, eyes glittering, "…I'll pick up your bike and throw it over that fucking wall. What do you think of that?"

I shrugged.

"Nothing to say?" He took a step towards the bike. I realised he might do it. He was enjoying himself too much.

The bike had been a present from my parents, the first time they'd been able to buy a new one. My eyes were watering and I was afraid to speak in case my voice betrayed me. I shrugged again.

The man spoke very slowly.

"I'm going to chuck your shitty bike over that wall and there's nothing you can do about it."

"I can take your number," I said. "I can phone the police."

There was silence. The man in the car leaned over to the window.

"Come on, Tel. The little cunt's going to start crying."

The man leaned in until his face was inches from mine. He stank. I wanted to pick up a rock, to smash it into his face, over and again until nothing was left. I stood motionless, frozen, eyes down.

"And I can throw you right after. Can't I?"

It was a long moment. He straightened and cuffed me round the head, harder this time and strolled back towards the car. I didn't look. The driver gunned the engine, the door slammed and with an explosion of gravel the car shot away. The woman was laughing in the rear window, her middle finger up.

Dust hung in the air. We stood in silence, wondering if they'd return.

I heard the scrape of Neil picking up his bike. I grabbed mine, determined to be first, peddling off without a glance back, hoping he hadn't seen my tears.

Somebody, I swore to myself, was going to catch it at school on Monday. Somebody else.

CHILDREN

The Pencil Case

The four of us sat around the thick beamed table in the science lab. I stared at the carved obscenities, astonished that anyone could be so daring, so bad. The first day of secondary school, all of us hunched, shifting eyes and half-smiles. Elliott I knew from primary school, fidgeting on his stool, thighs tight in black trousers. We are no longer friends. Mark, vacant, inscrutable. I have no idea what became of Mark. Jon, buzz cut and ears like a chimpanzee, twitching, glancing around, never at rest. Jon's dead now. He killed himself, unable to live with addiction. On the desk in front of us, ready for inspection, a pencil case, pristine, filled with sharpened pencils, fountain pens, rulers, rubbers, protractors, and, for stabbing each other in the back, compasses.

My pencil case was brown, a faux-leather oblong, zipped up tight. My grandparents had bought and stocked it for me. It was a good pencil case, better than the others', I thought, looking around. There were tin ones, set to be dented, wooden ones with sliding lids and hinges, indestructible but unwieldy, cloth ones with pictures, designs meant to reflect their owner's character: Manchester United, The A Team, Duran Duran, horses, and so on.

As the years went by, my pencil case endured as others fell: seams undone, hinge misaligned, zipper broken, or retired due to embarrassment. Mine was timeless: stylish and utilitarian. I looked after it in a way that I didn't with much of my stuff, perhaps because it was a gift from my grandparents. The exterior remained immaculate; the interior lining showed ink stains, but they didn't bleed through. It was a weird thing to be proud of, but I was.

As we grew older and more destructive, pencil cases were vandalised. Elliott's ironic Henry's Cat case would sport huge erections and pendulous testicles each time his back was turned. There were only so many times they could be erased before ghostly phallic outlines became indelible. Someone scrawled "gay rights now!" on Jon's pencil case, which was funny back then, to some of us. Maybe because it was brown and hard to mark, my case remained inviolable: felt-tip wiped off and the surface depressed under ball point so that it couldn't grip. But even those attempts to assail were rare. There was, on some level, respect.

By the GCSE year, it had attained almost mythic status. It was, to my knowledge, the only pencil case from day one, let alone year one, left standing. On the outside at least, it was almost as perfect as the day as it been given to me. It was the Dorian Gray of pencil cases. In our still short lives, it seemed to defy the passage of time, of the change that we saw in ourselves. Though we were still in the ascendancy, my pencil case seemed to give hope in the face of inevitable decline.

Until that day in Biology. The Bunsen burners were on, hissing blue and orange around the room. Elliott stared at me over the flame, a smile twisting his lips. He was heating something, holding it with pliers: a piece of wire. It began to glow red and then orange. I could not have anticipated such malice, could have done nothing to prevent it; the act was committed with such swiftness that it was not until I smelled hot plastic that I realised.

I snatched the pencil case away. A thin line was scored in the front, just below the zipper, a fissure with lips of melted latex, a keloid scar. There was nothing that could be done to put things right. It was over, the perfection, the immutability. I stared at the desecration and then up at Elliott. He looked away, smirking. He had made his mark.

A Journey by Train

Mama packed the bags days ago, but she won't let me tell anyone. She says people will be jealous, but I think she's worried about getting in trouble with school.

I can tell she's excited; she can't sit still and runs for the telephone every time it rings. It's never Papa though. He's not allowed to call. Mama can't wait to see him again. She says he's at the end of the journey. Two trains and a boat and then another train. I've never been on a big boat before. I keep asking when we're going but Mama gets angry and snaps that she doesn't know. I can't wait to see Papa. His face is starting to get blurry. I can remember his smell though, like leather and soap. A warm smell.

There's a knock at the door. She nearly jumps out of her skin. It's Peter. I have to call him Uncle Peter. He's not really my uncle.

"Get your bag," Mama tells me.

Halfway to the station I realise we've left Martha behind. Mama tells me it's too late, we'll have to leave her, but I start crying and Peter turns the car around.

"We should still make it," he says.

I don't go in to get Martha; Peter runs in and finds her on my bed. I say, "Thank you," and put her safely in my bag. I wonder if Mama's got Martha's ear – she still hasn't sewn it back on – but I don't dare ask.

Peter drives much faster this time and Mama keeps looking at her watch. I see Peter take her arm and squeeze it. I don't like that. I'll tell Papa.

Peter stops in front of the station and we get out. Peter has the tickets and he runs with us through the ticket hall to the platform. He tells the ticket-collector he's just carrying our bags. Mama keeps looking over her shoulder and Peter is sweating. The ticket-collector frowns but lets us through. Peter is bundling us into the carriage when a whistle blows, and I think the guard should have waited until the door was closed.

Then Peter is grabbed.

His eyes go wide as he disappears into a crowd of men. They're all wearing horrid black uniforms and shiny boots. One of them steps forward. His hands are behind his back and he's smiling but his eyes are like stones. Mama's hand starts squeezing mine so hard it hurts. Her hand is getting slippery. I can hear Peter shouting and then his voice stops in the middle of what he's saying. I can see him again. Two men are holding him on each side, dragging him down the platform like a big dolly. Some of the people on the platform have turned to watch but most are hurrying away, heads down. I reach inside my bag to make sure Martha's alright, squeezing her softness. The smiling man steps towards the train and holds out his hand. He's wearing black leather gloves. I can smell him now he's closer. Sausages and cigarettes.

"Perhaps Papa will come to us now," he says.

There's a skull on his hat. It's smiling.

A Tent on a Hill

The teacher's voice droned like a car stuck in the middle lane. Henry stared out of the window, his gaze resting on the horizon, not really focusing on anything, not really present, his mind floating. It was another grey day, both outside and in. He'd not slept well. His parents had been drinking and arguing till long after dark. No one had woken him in the morning, and he'd got a detention for being late. His mind sharpened as he began to wonder what state she'd be in when he got home.

The teacher's drone shifted gear.

"Henry! Do you think you might join us for a moment?!"

The class tittered. Henry apologised and faced front. Something had caught his eye though. What was it? He glanced back. Yes, there in a field, near the top of the hill was a tent, a white tent. What was it doing there?

The following day Henry had Geography again. The tent was still there. Geography was one of the only lessons he had on the third floor, high enough to have a view over the roof tops of the estate. It was another overcast day. Henry stared out of the window at the white apex that stood out against the green of grass and trees. Why would anyone put up a tent in the middle of the field? There were no roads or paths leading to it and he'd seen no one coming or going in all the time he'd been looking. Maybe the farmer was growing something in there.

"Henry!" The voice was more impatient, no longer joking. More like his mother. "Eyes front."

"Sorry, Miss."

The tent was still there the following lesson but this time the teacher ran out of patience.

"I don't know what's so fascinating out there, Henry, but you clearly need to be where its appeal cannot distract."

The Isolation Room was also on the third floor, but they'd put plastic frosting on the windows. Henry stared at a spot on the wall and hoped his mother was in a better mood when he got home. He didn't think it likely. She'd sent him an incoherent text message at lunchtime. In fact, when he got out of school he decided not to go home; he decided to hike up the hill and investigate the tent.

He cut through two fields – there was no footpath and he had to cross the gates – hoping the farmer wouldn't come and chase him off. The ground was firm; although the sky had been grey for days, there had been no rain. When he got to the field where the tent should have been, there was nothing there. He wondered if it could have been taken down while he was climbing up, but he didn't think it possible. He looked at the ground. There was no pale patch in the grass where a tent could have been. In fact, the grass of the pasture didn't look like anyone or anything had been on it for a long time. He crossed over the field to the right and then to the left, thinking he may have lost his bearings, but there was nothing. He went back to the first field. It was beginning to grow dark, but he didn't care, the longer he stayed out the better. He sat down and put a blade of grass between his teeth, gazing over the town, trying not to think.

Henry didn't have Geography again until the following week. The weather had improved and as Henry took his seat he looked out towards the horizon and saw that the tent was there again, only now it was blue. He laughed.

"Care to share Henry?" asked the teacher.

Henry shook his head.

"No Miss, just realised I've been a bit stupid."

The teacher raised her eyebrows.

"There's an admission."

Henry looked back to the little tent of blue where the field ended and the trees overarched to create the apex. He hadn't noticed the gap in the hedge when he'd been up there. He wondered what was on the other side. When school let out, he decided, he'd go up and find out. There might be a nice view on the other side.

The Butterfly Hook

The bell rang and Miss Monroe told us to get our coats from the hall. Everyone's coat hook had a different animal above it. Mine was a butterfly, only my coat wasn't on it. Even after everyone else had taken their coats I couldn't see mine. Miss Monroe came and helped. Someone had shoved it under the bench. Miss Monroe helped me put it on. I could smell her perfume, like posh soap. She was much nicer than my last teacher. Mrs Foster had funny green eyes that made me feel strange when I looked at her. She smelled of meat. Miss Monroe was much nicer. She held my hand as we walked outside and down the path to the gate. It was cold and icy. Mums and dads were waiting, hugging their children and taking them home. Except mine. She was always late. I'd only been at the school four days and she'd never been on time.

"Can you see Mummy?" asked Miss Monroe. The cold was making my eyes watery. I shook my head.

Time went by and most of the parents and children had gone. Miss Monroe's hand was warm but my other hand was cold.

Soon it was just us.

"Shall we go back inside?"

I nodded.

Just then Mum arrived. She grabbed my hand and walked off really fast. I had to run to keep up.

"Bye Jake," Miss Monroe called. "See you tomorrow."

I didn't have breath to reply.

Mum put me in the car and drove away. I put the seat belt on myself. If I wished hard enough, I wondered, maybe Miss Monroe could be my mum.

Elliott's Lie

I didn't see it, but I wished I had. It sounded hilarious the way Elliott described it: Ryan Gordon's mother driving at full speed around the estate, screaming at Mr Gordon who was on the bonnet, hanging on to the windscreen-wipers for dear life, screaming at her to pull over. Then she jammed on the brakes and he flew off, bouncing along the road.

Ryan was a weedy kid, the kind who got stick but made it worse by saying stupid stuff. His mother didn't help letting his curly hair grow in a helmet round his lolly-pop head. It probably looked cute when he was six, but he was nearly a teenager.

When I told Mum she didn't think it was funny.

"How awful," she said, but I didn't get it; I thought she was being goody-goody, that she was in one of her Christian phases. How could anyone not find it funny? Elliott and I had been practically crying with laughter. Elliott hated Ryan. There were rumours about Elliott's mum and Ryan's dad. They were rubbish of course, Elliott said.

If only Mum had taken the time to tell me *why* it was awful, to ask me how I'd have felt if it had been her driving *my* dad around the estate… I'd probably still have laughed. But I might have got it.

On the following Monday back in school, I asked Ryan. Instead of getting the embarrassment and humiliation I'd hoped for, Ryan just looked blank as if he'd no idea what I was talking about. He wasn't a good liar, but

I preferred to believe it had really happened. I didn't want the joke falling flat.

Elliott wouldn't have lied to me.

Her Voice

Her voice cut slowly through his consciousness. He opened his eyes to find her standing over him. Sunlight glared behind the curtains.

"Daddy."

The TV was playing. He was on the sofa, fully clothed. Shit. His skull contracted and he winced. He wondered if he could sit up without wanting to be sick.

"Daddy!" There was panic in her voice. He forced his eyes to focus. She was in her pyjamas, tugging at his sleeve. "Santa didn't come."

Oh shit… He hauled himself upright, trying to think, brain swimming. He could remember wrapping them the night before. He must have passed out waiting for her to go to sleep. Should have stuck to beer.

"Have I been a bad girl, Daddy?"

Fuck, fuck.

Her eyes were shining. She blinked and wiped them on her sleeve. Her bottom lip wobbled.

Where had he left them?

"No, my love, of course not. You're the *best* girl." He pulled her close, horrified for a moment, thinking he might vomit down her back. She smelled sweet, like strawberries. Shit. Think, *think*.

She pulled away, wrinkling her nose.

"Why didn't he come?"

Think.

It came to him.

"He thought you were at Mummy's, so he left the presents there. When he realised he'd made a mistake, he called me."

"Santa called you? On a phone?"

He nodded.

"Uh huh. And I had to go and get the presents."

He remembered now, they were in his bedroom in a bin-liner. Relief surged through him.

"You got the presents?!" Her face lit up before collapsing to a frown. "But you left me here? On my own?"

"No, no. Santa sent an elf. He stayed while I went to get them."

She narrowed her eyes.

"You left me with an elf?"

"Yes." He coughed. "Now listen, you want your presents, right? And you want to spend Christmas with me again?" She nodded. "Well, that stuff I told you, about Santa and the elf and stuff. You must *never* tell Mummy, OK?"

Her eyes narrowed again.

"Why?"

He sighed. Perhaps a shower would help. It was going to be a long day.

The Conjuror

Sawyers let us into the lab and we took our seats. A Bunsen burner, clamp and some other devices were set up at the front. I could tell Sawyers was excited and after he got us quiet, he started to introduce the lesson.

I'd never liked him; he blamed me for anything that went wrong and was always smarming over the girls. He smelled damp and wore home-made ties. And he had a moustache.

As he talked, I noticed him patting the pockets of his lab coat and then, after finding nothing, he crossed to where his tweed jacket was draped over the chair behind his desk. He reached inside and extracted something, palming it. No one seemed to have noticed.

Sidling up to Susan Austin he leaned in and as she recoiled, produced a cigarette from behind her ear. Amidst laughter and catcalls he lit the fag and placed it in the clamp.

"We'll leave it there for a minute and see how much tar we collect," he smiled. "So some of you can see the state your lungs will be getting in."

The smell of smoke filled the room.

Sawyers began talking again and then, pretending to have forgotten a prop, told us to behave for a minute while he went to the prep room to fetch it. He swept from the room unable to conceal a smirk.

The room was silent.

"Go on Corker," someone stage-whispered, "have a drag."

The class erupted with encouragement.

Corker brayed with laughter, turning red.

"No way."

"Go on."

Corker looked at the door and seeing no-one, got up from his stool and ran to the front of the room. All eyes were on him.

"Don't do it," I whispered. "He's watching from the prep room." Corker hesitated, torn, the class baying, before returning to his seat.

Sawyers stalked back into the room glaring at me. The lesson continued, the room stinking as he showed how much tar had been collected.

As we filed out of the class at the end, I wondered how long it would be before Sawyers realised the pack of Rothmans had vanished from his blazer.

The Last Days of the Edwards Gang

Gareth came up with the idea; he usually did. He'd been picking up stones as we made our way through the estate, bouncing them in his palm, filling his pockets, and as we approached the bridge, I assumed he was planning on chucking them at the factory windows. It was great, the smash and tinkle when you threw a good one, but there weren't many panes left, only the higher ones and they were harder to get.

Whatever we did over those long hot summers, Gareth lead and we followed. Eddie and I started picking up our own stones.

When we got to the bridge, instead of crossing, Gareth stopped and turned to us with the lopsided grin that always made me nervous and excited at the same time. Something was going to happen.

"What are you going to do?"

He held a finger to his lips and narrowed his eyes, looking first one way, then the other. It was the main line between London and Swansea, so we didn't have to wait long. First the distant toot of a horn and then the slowly building growl of the engine until the yellow front appeared around the curve of the track.

I could see the driver's eyes. He must have known what we were up to, and he sounded the horn again. As the train bellowed under us in a cloud of grey diesel, Gareth began flinging his stones at the curved grey roof, his eyes wild, face contorted in a grin. The stones hit like gun shots and cannoned off in different directions, one even clanging like a bullet against the steel structure of the bridge.

"Shit!" I screamed. "Stop it! That nearly hit us." Gareth laughed and carried on flinging the stones.

When the train had passed, he was panting, face red and eyes glinting. Eddie and I still had our hands full of stones. Gareth glanced around both ends of the bridge, checking for adults.

"Come on," he said, "let's go and take out the windows."

We returned a couple more times and both times Eddie and I joined in. All good fun, but on the fourth occasion Gareth went too far. As we were walking through the estate, he spotted a wrought iron gate, fly-tipped in an alley.

"Check this out! Imagine the noise it'll make!"

"Don't be stupid," Eddie said. "That could go through the roof. It could kill someone."

"Don't be a pussy. Help me carry it."

Eddie shook his head.

Gareth made me do it. I even helped him heave it up onto the edge of the bridge. We were lucky, the first train to pass came on our side of the tracks.

"Don't do it," pleaded Eddie.

"Wait till the driver's past," whispered Gareth, his eyes unblinking. "We don't want it going through the cab."

The noise of the gate striking the train was like a bomb going off, loud even above the scream of the horn.

We rushed to the other side of bridge. The train carried on, its grey haze enveloping us.

"Look at the dent!" cried Gareth.

"Boys," said Eddie, his voice strangely flat. He hadn't followed us over to the other side of the bridge. "The gate's on the track."

We crossed back over. He was right, the gate had bounced off the train and come to rest on the westbound rails.

"We've got to get it off," said Eddie. "It'll derail a train."

"Fuck that," said Gareth, his face pale. "It'll just push it out the way."

Eddie shook his head and looked at us both. When he saw we weren't going to help, he turned and ran off the bridge the way we'd come. Gareth and I looked at each other, our ears straining for the sound of a train. All I could hear was the tinny sound of a radio somewhere on the estate. It was playing Queen.

Eddie appeared out of the undergrowth and glanced in both directions. The sound of a horn came from the east.

"Get back!" screamed Gareth, waving his arm. I saw Eddie muttering under his breath. He stepped out, over the first rail and onto the sleepers. I looked over my shoulder. The train hadn't appeared, but I could hear its approach. It was an express. I turned back. Eddie was struggling with the gate. He wasn't a big lad and his face was red, contorted with effort. I realised that if we'd all gone down, or just one of us, we'd have been able to get it off.

The horn screamed, not the usual two tones, but a long blast.

"EDDIE!"

He looked up, saw the train, looked back at the gate, tried once more to shift it and then scrambled back over the rails. The horn wailed. The train hit and noise filled the world. Eddie disappeared. The train reared, buckling as it bounced on, slewing to the side, no longer secure on its tracks, the wheels screaming with friction.

We didn't wait to see what happened, we ran. But as we ran, we could hear it, a terrible rending, a shriek that seemed go on and on.

And then it stopped.

All I could hear was the sound of my trainers slapping the pavement and my panting breath.

What had we done?

Somewhere a radio was playing.

The next morning Dad read his newspaper at the breakfast table.

"Two people killed on that train yesterday. They say here it was kids put metal railings on the track." He looked up and pointed his fork at me, his mouth full of bacon. "If I ever hear of you doing anything like that, I'll make sure you don't walk straight for a week. You're not to go anywhere near that bloody railway. Understand?"

I nodded, cradling my tea, praying that Eddie wouldn't split.

CRIME

All That I've Done

There was only one I didn't kill straight away. He was crying, on his knees, saying, "God help me, God help me," that kind of thing, so I thought, why not, see what happens. So I told him he had half an hour, to see if God would show up and, you know, change the circumstances.

He stayed on his knees, his eyes closed and his lips moving. I could barely hear what he was saying. His brow was furrowed, like he was really concentrating, willing it to happen.

I smoked and watched. He was kneeling in a puddle. His grey trousers were dark down one leg. I was interested to see if anything happened, what it would mean for me, given all that I've done.

At the end of the half-hour God hadn't shown up and the circumstances hadn't changed. He started praying faster but it didn't make any difference.

It wasn't pretty. That's the only one I regret, for how I did it. I shouldn't have done it like that. I shouldn't have given him that time.

Donovan's Error

There was something about Donovan Lear that intrigued Chef de Partie, Andrew Woodhouse. Both were smokers and Woodhouse made sure they took their coffee breaks at the same time. Lear was flattered and confused by the attention.

Woodhouse watched Lear as he scrubbed away at stubborn sauce marks on crockery and pans, fascinated and repelled by his reptilian presence. He noted the waitresses avoiding the new man, despite him doing nothing to justify their aversion.

After a couple of days, Woodhouse was giving Lear lifts to and from work, careful not to let his colleagues see them arrive or depart together. No one else spoke with Lear so there was little chance of anyone finding out. Lear lived in a crummy flat near the canal. Woodhouse hadn't seen anyone around during the pickups or drop-offs. Lear seemed to be the only resident of the whole run-down district.

The other chefs mocked Lear, and Woodhouse joined them in the teasing. Lear would smile at Woodhouse, hoping he might be in on the jokes he failed to understand. The others noticed the smiles and joked that Lear fancied Woodhouse. Woodhouse laughed along.

Woodhouse – Woodlouse to his colleagues – began probing Lear, discussing drugs, pornography, seeing what Lear would disclose, encouraging him when he showed interest in anything remotely deviant. Lear, desperate to impress, soon revealed that he'd beaten to death a young barmaid who'd spurned his advances. Lear had hidden in the toilets when she'd been closing up and attacked her when everyone else had gone. He'd bundled her body into the broom closet and left. He'd been arrested within twenty-four hours.

Woodhouse was impressed; he'd not expected such a revelation. He'd been expecting some sort of sex crime, child molestation or rape. Lear, he discovered, had served ten years before being granted parole. This was his first job.

Having always been interested in killing, Woodhouse quizzed Lear about the crime and was both thrilled and sickened by the fire in Lear's eyes as he recounted and relived the young woman's last moments. Woodhouse had always wondered what it would be like to take another's life, and in Lear he saw an opportunity. One evening, on the way home from a shift, he stopped the car and suggested they smoke a joint by the canal. Woodhouse did not inhale a great deal but watched as Lear grew glassy-eyed. When Lear leaned over and tried to kiss him, any concerns Woodhouse had over a guilty conscience evaporated. He pushed Lear over on his side and digging his hands into Lear's hair and bashed his head on the curb-stone until he heard the skull crunch. Glancing around, he rolled Lear into the canal where he floated face down and drifted away.

When the body was recovered the next day, it was presumed he'd slipped and fallen in. Toxicology tests seemed to confirm this. The police didn't even interview Woodhouse. In fact, the killing had been so easy, it wasn't long before he started wondering how he might do another.

The Drunk

I left the pub before closing time – the beer wasn't agreeable – and cut through the park. It wasn't a great idea, and I only did it because I'd had a few. The centre of the park was far from roads and screened by trees; cries for help went unnoticed. There had been a number of muggings and rapes over the years.

I climbed the steps to the raised circular mesa where the long-gone bandstand once stood. The night was still and almost silent. I was just about to descend the steps on the far side when I saw, at the bottom, a body sprawled on the concrete. A man, apparently unconscious.

As I peered into the gloom beyond the halo of lamplight, I stopped, wary of ambush. With slow steps I descended towards the prone body. I kept glancing around, into the darkness. The man appeared to be breathing. A slug of yellow phlegm hung on his cheek. He was in his mid-twenties, blond-haired and bearded, like a dissolute Viking.

"Hey," I said nudging him with my toe.

Nothing.

I leaned in and shook his shoulder. "Hey," I said again, louder this time. His eyes rolled open.

"Eurgh."

He staggered to his feet, reeling, the coordination of his torso – which stayed perfectly upright, assisted by flailing arms – seemingly independent of his legs which, knock-kneed, careened first in one direction and then another. Pitching over backwards, he landed on his arse, momentum rolling him onward so that his head cracked on concrete.

Christ, I thought, he's going to have a bleed on the brain. I knew if I left him, he might die, or someone might go through his pockets.

This will be a story, I thought, something to tell in the pub. I wondered how it would end, if it would be me who decided its conclusion. Was I to be the hero or even the protagonist?

I hauled him to his feet ensuring his snotty cheek was on the other side.

"What's your name?"

He turned and peered at me, confused.

"Josh."

"Where do you live Josh?"

He gave me an address on the nearby estate.

"Let's go."

It took us four times longer than it should to get where we were going, me trying to steer and cajole him, keeping him upright. He was suspicious at first, wanting to know why I was helping, then horribly grateful, crying in gratitude, telling me what a good person I was, that most people wouldn't have done it.

In my heart I knew he was right, but I hated to admit it. I couldn't help congratulating myself on my charity, despite knowing that to do so negated the selflessness of the act.

He asked about my life, and I told him a bit, but not too much. It was good, I thought, to keep him talking. He told me how lucky I was, and I agreed, never having thought about it much before. Compared to him I was lucky. He was a recovering heroin addict among other things. All the while I tried to keep our physical contact to the minimum, mindful of the snot, the possibility of vomit and the suspicion that he might have pissed himself.

After half an hour and several wrong turns, we found ourselves outside his front door. I wanted to knock to let his landlord know he was in and that he might want to keep an eye on his pissed-up lodger, but he begged me not to. They'd evict him, he said, and I realised this was probably not the first time something like this had happened.

He found his key and I shepherded him inside, accepted his thanks and made sure the door was closed behind him. I made my way down the steps to the pavement and watched through the frosted glass as he lurched up the stairs to the landing. He seemed to have sobered up a little.

I walked home at a brisk pace, eager to wash my hands. I vowed to tell no-one.

Cul-de-Sac

She was the last to arrive. Most people moved in the day the builders handed the keys over, but her house stayed empty for a couple of weeks. She was renting which probably explains it. We still don't know who owns the place, even after everything that's happened.

She was certainly pretty, there's no taking that away from her, and polite. But not particularly friendly. She didn't come around for Christmas drinks at Elaine's or come to Brian's when he set up the Neighbourhood Watch. That didn't set any alarm bells ringing, but it did raise a few eyebrows. I think some of the women weren't that keen. She was pretty and got attention, but that wasn't really her fault. It wasn't something she set out to do. In fact, when she left the house, which wasn't often, she was usually in joggers and a hoodie. No make-up.

It was the cars that kept turning up that made us wonder. Posh cars – BMWs, Audis – that sort of thing, and at funny times of the day and night. They'd pull into her drive and a man would get out – it was always a man – and head straight to the front door which she'd open without him having to knock. I was the first to notice, but when I mentioned it at the next meeting a few others said they'd noticed but hadn't really *noticed* it. After that, they *did* start noticing it.

Brian started doing a bit of research online and, when he found out, he called an emergency meeting in his front room. He had his laptop open and showed us what he'd found.

Luscious Lucinda. That was what she called herself. You never saw her face in the pictures, just her body, nice body it was, not too skinny, wearing slinky underwear and high heels. In one picture she was draped over the sofa, in another she was bending over the kitchen table, then, in yet another, she was going up the stairs. Everywhere but the bedroom come to think of it. It didn't leave much to the imagination. My Justin wondered if she'd do a discount for locals. I could have killed him. A couple of the men laughed but I gave them a glare and that shut them up. Cheryl wanted to know how we knew Luscious Lucinda was her next door when we couldn't see her face. Gareth suggested making an appointment and went very red when no-one spoke. Right to the tips of his ears. "No need for that," said Brian tapping the screen. "Look at the house. Look at the décor." He was right, we all had the same beige carpet and magnolia walls that the builders put in. And the layout of the house was the same, only the mirror of our house, but still, it was the same as Brian's. She had the lace curtains pulled so you couldn't see outside, but the clincher was the front door which she was pretending to open, starkers, in one picture. It had the same stained-glass panels as every house on the cul-de-sac.

We went over, not all of us – me, Brian, Justin, Elaine, and Patsy – and told her she had to pack it in, that it wasn't on in a quiet residential street. First, she acted all innocent, but when Brian told her about his research, she told us where to go in no uncertain terms. Most unladylike.

It was Elaine's idea. Every time we saw a car pulling up, we'd go out and take pictures on our phones and then stand outside banging pots and pans. That dampened their ardour. Cheeky bitch even called the police on us once. Anyway, it did the trick and she moved out after a week.

I heard she's doing the same thing in Droitwich now. Brian found her. I think he's turning into a bit of a cyber-stalker.

A load of Asian lads moved in last week. They keep themselves to themselves and don't make any trouble. No strange comings and goings. Justin says they're Vietnamese, though God knows how he knows that. He said they won't have any snow on their roof come the winter, whatever that means. It's probably something racist.

Just Do It

Remi lit a cigarette and moved to the window. Below, on the opposite side of the street, an old man in a sheepskin coat was emerging from the Tesco Metro.

Remi's phone buzzed. As he reached into his pocket he glanced at Steve. Steve made a strangled sound through his gag. He was in his underpants, tied to a chair, nose bloody.

Remi cupped his hand behind his ear.

"What's that? Can't hear you mate."

Steve's eyes were huge and wet.

Remi opened the message. It was the code word. He was glad; he'd had enough.

Outside the old man stopped by a bin and took something from his pocket: a scratch card. Remi watched him take a coin and work at the silver, revealing the numbers, tight with anticipation. Remi couldn't stand it, watching someone do a scratch card. There was something awful about it. The dream, the momentary pleasure in the possibility that life might improve. He hated it, the lack of dignity, the false hope. There was nothing more depressing. For a moment the man was motionless, checking, double checking. Remi could almost see the last grains of delusion running out, the inevitable realisation as the shoulders slumped. The man tossed the card to the ground and shuffled away, breath white in the cold air. Remi noticed he was wearing slippers. Loser. Buying disappointment. Why did he bother?

Surely he knew it was nearly all over? Remi stubbed his cigarette on the sill and sighed.

Funny, he thought turning to Steve. That was exactly what he liked to see when he was working. The hope. The hope in their eyes. It made it so much more... worthwhile.

He looked at the message again.

NIKE.

Jackpot. He looked into Steve's pleading eyes and smiled. Steve wet himself.

Tip

I grew up in a market town in the west of England. Material poverty wasn't prevalent, quite the opposite for the most part, but poverty of the imagination was. It didn't help that there was little to do other than drink. On weekends the pavements of the town centre were starred with glass and splashed with blood and vomit. Many preferred to stay at home.

PizzaZ did good trade, delivering sweaty deep pans to the estates and beyond. I did this for a while, flat boxes stinking up my car, knocking on smoky doors behind which big dogs barked. The poorer the house the better the tip.

On my first night, the boss sent me out with Gareth to learn the ropes. He talked non-stop, charming the doorsteps with flirty banter, eyes swivelling all over the place, through curtain cracks, into hallways and living rooms.

Gareth smelled of weed and cologne, a heady mix that battled the pizza and Magic Tree in his wide wheeled Peugeot 206. We drove the narrow streets with the windows down and sub-woofer booming. For a pizza delivery boy, he was well-turned out: Armani and Aqua Scutum. While he may have been quick of wit, Gareth was not what you'd called nuanced.

He'd been threatened a few times and the police had paid a visit but found nothing. Gareth may have had sharp eyes, but the light fingers belonged to someone else. Spoils were shared.

One night Tony took a call for a big house out of town. Gareth took the

61

delivery, drove down the lanes, past the gates and up the drive. The tweedy bloke who answered the door wasn't expecting him. They argued for a while, but he wasn't paying for what he hadn't ordered. With a single fingered salute, Gareth spun on the gravel and was gone.

When he got to the bottom of the drive, he found the gates closed. They'd been open when he arrived, and he certainly hadn't shut them after he'd gone through. He stepped out of the car and into the darkness.

When the police found him later that night, the engine was still running, exhaust fogging the beams of the headlights. Gareth had been dumped in the bracken, his face unrecognisable. He never woke up and eventually his mother had him switched off.

No one's ever been charged but there are plenty of rumours, plenty of names.

Burglaries went down overnight.

INDUSTRY

Glospak

Dense cloud smothered the town, drizzling on the predawn pavements and blurring the streetlight. In damp hands cupped against biting wind, I lit a cigarette and exhaled a cloud that whipped away before it could form. Over the eastern hills a cold line of sun filtered through the cloud.

"Get on with it," shouted Gary from the warehouse. "You can smoke on your break."

I flicked the cigarette away, lowered the visor and picked up the hose. Gary laughed and disappeared inside. I was wearing overalls too thin for the season and rain was running down my collar. I took a negative from the pile – thick acetate sheets, two foot by three, used to print images on plastic boxes – leaned it against the warehouse wall and turned on the pressure hose. Water thundered, wind blowing spray back in my face, turning the visor to a kaleidoscope. I moved the jet across the surface, erasing an image of flowers, yellow peonies. It had been for a consignment of cosmetics, not one box of which would have been opened, I was sure, with a single thought for how it had been produced, for me…

Could life, I wondered, get any worse?

Inside, the machines would be grinding on, over and over, picking up the sheets of hand-fanned plastic, heating them, folding them, gluing them, spewing them onto tables to be stacked and then boxed and then, when each box was filled, to be stacked in its turn. The only relief was a jam, two sheets going through instead of one and the plastics piling up, melting on the hot plates. Quick! Hit the button, open the cage, pull them out, fingers red with burns. The noise of machines beat a syncopated rhythm that echoed on the walls. Radio 1 played behind it all, a mad cacophony. The air was fuzzy with static. Fat bluebottles cruised, strangely slow, through chasms of stacked boxes, high on the fumes of heated plastic and glue. Lids and boxes would come on and on, concertinaed into stacks, into boxes, more and more, into boxes, more, more, tape the box, stack the box, get back to the table, the lids are piling, the lids are piling, get it under control…

The alarm woke me, and I slammed it off with an outstretched hand. It was dark and I could hear rain on the window. I had been dreaming of the factory, I had been there, stacking boxes, over and over. I'd worked there the evening before, a ten-hour shift; it had wormed in my head. How long had I dreamed it? All six hours? And I hadn't even been paid. And now another ten.

Gary came into the tea-room where we sat drinking instant coffee from plastic cups. "Right," he said, clapping his hands, smiling. "Who wants machines, and which lucky bastard wants the hose?"

I raised my hand. Anything but the machines.

MEDICAL

Mr Happy

"Get up. You're going to school. Your grandfather invaded Sicily with dysentery."

"What? On his own?"

"I'm not telling you again."

So my stoicism was installed for future trials. Inside my trenches packages of love and lies would arrive, blessed with kisses and hopes for life.

After numerous hints, delivered like merciful blows, she finally stopped buying me boxer shorts with Mr Happy of the Mr Men emblazoned on the leg.

It was easier after that, no more waking thinking, "Christ, what next?" and then opening my smalls drawer and seeing that yellow fool waiting his turn with a smile.

Halo

The first I knew about it was the itch, a nagging burn at the top of my thigh. I went up to the bathroom and pulled down my trousers and pants to have a look. There, just to the right of my pubes was a mark, a red nipple, the skin angry and peeling around the lump. That doesn't look good, I thought, that's not a normal bite. Whatever made that needed to be got rid of pronto. I locked the door and took my pants off.

I found it quickly. At first, I thought it was another bite, a red lump *under* the skin of my scrotum. I squeezed and it hurt more than it ought, so I looked closer. It was under the skin, about the size of a fennel seed, dark red and swollen. I squeezed again. The pain seemed to come from under the lump, not at the sides where I was putting pressure. I realised this wasn't another bite, *this* was the culprit.

A friend had once told me about finding a tick on his balls. He'd also told me what he'd done to remove it, though that part of the story eluded me now that I most needed the information. It occurred to me that what was happening would be funny if it wasn't happening to me.

I knew there were various methods of removing ticks, application of flame, smothering in grease, but that they all ran the risk of increased problems, the louse burrowing deeper, or the head being left inside the body. I also didn't fancy waving a flame around my nut sack. Still, I needed the bastard gone straight away; I wasn't having anything drinking the blood out of my balls for a second longer than I had to. Without pausing to think too much about it, I reached for the tweezers.

With a slight pressure the tick exploded, blood splashing my thighs and running down my scrotum; it was immensely satisfying. I pulled the tick from under the skin and then took some toilet paper and held it to the wound. After a minute or so I swapped the blood-soaked tissue for another and then, after a minute, replaced the tissue again. And then again after a minute more.

I decided it might be a good idea to lie down.

My wife found me five minutes later.

"What are you doing?"

"My balls won't stop bleeding."

The tick must have used an anticoagulant; there was a small mound of bloody tissues by the side of the bed.

"Could you get me a plaster?"

She laughed. "You don't want to do that. Imagine taking it off."

I told her I didn't mind. I was a tough guy.

When I checked the plaster half an hour later it had bled through onto my boxer shorts, but it seemed to have stopped.

Later that evening I went outside to smoke a cigarette in the garden. I started worrying about Lyme disease, wondering if the tick's head was still stuck inside my ball-bag. I'd read that a high percentage of ticks carried it. John Lurie had Lyme disease, so did Amy Tan. How had they caught it? Did they get bitten on the balls? I was beginning to get carried away. Was that the beginning of a headache I was feeling? Aches in the joints? Would I become feverish? I decided that standing around smoking was a bad idea. It let me think too much. I went inside and watched TV.

Later that night I went back outside to smoke another cigarette. Around the moon was a halo, soft light emanating to a bright hard ring of light. I gazed up. I'd read about this sort of thing, ice particles in the atmosphere. A perfectly natural phenomena, I told myself. It was real, and I was seeing it. I held a hand to my forehead and, relieved that it felt cool, took another drag on my cigarette.

PSYCHOLOGY

Nemesis

I know as soon as I see him that I've met him before, that it wasn't a pleasant encounter. I'm in the park with my kids and he's there with his, or perhaps they're his nephews. The presence of children is probably a good thing; the animosity is instant and palpable. I'm on a bench; he's walking past and as our eyes lock, a mutual distaste and confusion passes between us: instant, visceral.

Our gaze holds for a moment too long, almost a challenge.

We've met somewhere, but I can't say where, only that it almost came to blows, violence dodged. It's a scene from a dream, just out of reach, a word on the tip of the tongue, an itch in the middle of the back. I can see his face: cheeky chappy, dimpled cheeks. The sort of face that thinks it can get away with anything, the sort of face that appeals to a dim sort of woman. A liar's face. I see it twisted in hatred, mocking with sneers, and fear he may have bested me. As he passes the urge to violence wells like oil. He is still fucking grinning, grinning at something his companion has said, but he's looking me in the eye and he's grinning and I know he knows, that he remembers, but I sense that he too cannot quite place it. There is something between us that no one else in the park shares. We have a connection.

Where was it? A pub? On the road? The violence mere moments away… This mist of remembrance, was it chemical? Alcoholic? Caused by a blow? No. The slogging of time and the years? Perhaps this is just a foretaste of things to come. Perhaps this is what happens when you're older. Best not to think of it.

He is almost past, still staring, still smiling. It could have been years ago. We both know something happened just not what. Still united in desire to do the other down. To see blood and bone for reasons unknown. The feeling is enough. I can smell it on him.

ROMANCE

In the First Place

Beryl says it's my own fault, which is just about typical. What did I expect? she says, a man of my age acting like that.

We were walking back from Morrisons, our weekly visit. We always have a cake and a cuppa in the café. It was a lovely day. Anyway, we were walking back when these three lads started calling out. At first, we didn't realise they were shouting at us. We thought they were just rowdy lads having a laugh, the way young people do nowadays. You know the sort, baseball caps on backwards. Why don't they just buy round hats? Anyway, they were sat on the wall opposite the Texaco, swigging from bottles of beer. It was only two o'clock. They can't have been more than sixteen. No school, no job, so where do they get the money for beer? Anyway, they started calling out, "baldy", "slaphead", that sort of thing. Beryl started talking to me in a loud voice, going on about our Michael coming over for tea with baby Josh, but she wasn't talking naturally, she was nervous and was trying to distract me. I wasn't having any of that. I dropped my bags. I looked over and caught the eye of one of them and there was no doubt who they were talking about. That was what I needed, certainty. Then I was gone. Off to get 'em.

"Come back," she called but I was already over the road.

They started laughing when they saw me coming, acting scared, but, you know, they were taking the piss. I went up to the biggest and started having a go. It's usually better that way, take out the ringleader and the others lose their bottle. Anyway, I was having a go, and he was saying, "Calm down Granddad," that sort of thing, and his mates were laughing, and that made me angrier. I could hear Beryl calling and she was trying to get across the road. She'd left her trolley, but she couldn't get over as there was so much traffic. Some of it slowed down to watch.

Anyway, I was jabbing my finger in this lad's face, and he was starting to get wound up. He could see I meant business, didn't like to be told what a little berk he actually was. Berk. Berkshire Hunt. You know. Nobody has the bottle to stand up to these little sods anymore and they end up running the estates. He didn't expect me to stand up to him and he didn't expect me to poke him in the eye. I hadn't meant to. I think one of his pals shoved him, but anyway, my finger went right in his eyeball. That stopped him. He screamed like a girl and bent double. I remember what I said then. I said, "Oops'" How daft is that? I nearly said sorry but then I remembered why I was there in the first place, and I felt really glad I'd done it, even if it was an accident. He was swearing like a sailor, calling me an effing C and all the rest of it.

It was then his mates started getting agitated. They'd gone all quiet after I'd poked their mate. They weren't sure what had happened at first and then they weren't sure what to do. They weren't the brightest boys but when they woke up, they got quite nasty.

Beryl was over the road by this time and was trying to pull me away, but I wasn't going anywhere. Quite a crowd had gathered by that point. I hadn't noticed with all that was going on and then suddenly, pow! There they were. One of the boys was poking me in the chest and saying, "Come on then, come on then," as though I was going to fight him. He was calling me a bastard and every name you could think of. None of the crowd were doing anything, just gawping, enjoying the spectacle. Couple of big men there as well. Did nothing, just watched. The other lad was shouting at me and trying to help his mate, the one with the eye, but then when Beryl came over, he called her a "bald bitch" and that made me lose it. That was why I was over there in the first place. I know how much it upsets her. She doesn't need some dickhead making her feel even worse just so him and his mates can have a laugh.

I saw red at that point and that punch was no accident. I used to box in the army, and I've still got a bit of it in me. It knocked him back a step. Beryl shrieked at me, "Gordon!" and that distracted me, made me drop my guard, turn to the left. The bugger was straight back at me, punched me on the nose, from the side. I heard it crunch and I went right over, sideways and backwards. Luckily, I missed Beryl, but I hit the ground hard. I heard it go, my hip.

That scared them, they must have heard it too, it was like the crack of a pistol. They took off like rabbits, even the one with the swollen eye.

A motorist stopped and it was him that called the ambulance. That's how I ended up in hospital. Beryl's alright though. I just hope it didn't bother her too much.

Women

"Jesus, Libby," shouted Max, shutting off the smoke alarm, taking the pan off the hob and opening the back door. "What are you playing at?" From the living room came a cheer from the TV echoed by a cheer from their son Kieran. "Christ! Now they've scored. Can't you even cook fucking dinner? I've worked an eleven hour day."

"Sorry."

"Sorry? Well, perhaps it would help if you'd put that bloody wine down." He stopped, hand on hips, breathing hard and staring. She was sitting at the table, gazing at her phone. He cocked his head. "Are you OK?"

She'd found out several days after it happened. On the Monday he didn't show up for their meeting and then he didn't return her calls. She wondered if she'd done something wrong. It went on for two days until his wife picked up, her voice hollow and flat, demanding to know who Libby was. Eventually, Libby couldn't stand it any longer and drove over to the house, something he'd forbidden her to do.

At first, she thought there was a party going on, then she realised most of the guests were wearing black.

He'd been so kind, so attentive, so loving. But now he was gone. She didn't even know how or why. She couldn't even say goodbye.

"Libby?"

She looked up and gave him a tired smile. "I'm fine. Just a long day. Shall I call a takeaway?"

Kieran appeared in the doorway. "Half-time. What's up with Mum? She's been weird all day."

Max waved his hand in the air. "I dunno. Women."

Fast Train to Burton

As he emerged from the subway, George shaded his eyes, blinking into the morning sun. At the top of the steps he paused, glancing around the island platform. It was busy and the benches all seemed taken. A little further on he found a space between a middle-aged woman and a gnarled old man. It wasn't hard to see why the space was free, but George's head was spinning and he had to sit down. He nodded as the man's yellowed eyes met his for an instant. The man folded his newspaper to make space before hunching his shoulders and continuing to read.

"Thanks."

The man grunted. He smelled of cigarettes and dirty linen. George turned and breathed through his mouth. He wondered if he should eat something to steady his stomach. He needed to sort himself out before he got to Portsmouth. Before he got back to Lydia.

A train pulled in and the woman to George's left got up and boarded. The man stayed where he was, nodding over his paper. As people hurried to and fro, George contemplated moving along the bench to the free space, but there was an arm-rest to his side and he'd have to get up to change positions. He didn't want to seem rude or make the old man feel bad. Not that he seemed the type to care much.

As the train pulled out the man coughed, a wet rattling sound. George knew he'd missed his opportunity. If he got up now it would seem too obvious. Glancing at his watch, he saw there were only ten minutes to go. He could endure. George reached inside his bag and pulled out a Coke. The bottle hissed and he held it at arm's length, the bubbles surging to the top. In his peripheral vision George saw the man turn to look, the newspaper falling to his lap.

The bottle settled just in time and George took a drink before recapping the bottle and controlling a burp.

The day ahead held fear and excitement. He was going to dump Lydia. The inevitable had happened the night before. He and Amelia had been dancing around each other for months, both literally and metaphorically. He'd expected to feel bad but, despite the hangover, he didn't. Rather he felt jubilant, which seemed to be smothering any feelings of guilt. At last he would be free, free to be with the girl he loved.

God, it was good to be alive.

But still, he felt bad about Lydia. It wasn't her fault. They should have known a long-distance relationship wouldn't work. He sighed. Best to think of it like taking a plaster off. Do it quickly. The pain would be over in an instant.

A meaty smell wafted into his nostrils. Jesus, the old boy had farted. George really had to move now. There was a long snorty rattle from the man. He was asleep. It was George's chance to move.

Just as George was about to get up, he felt the solid weight of the man's head slump onto his shoulder. The physical contact made him start and shudder. The greasy hair on the suede of his jacket! What should he do now?

The Tannoy announced the next train would not be stopping and that passengers should stand behind the yellow line. George thought of a meme he'd seen of a sign in a station, an old one from the eighties: "Passengers should keep away from the edge of the platform to avoid being sucked off". He almost laughed and then remembered where he was.

As the train approached, George shoved the man, hoping to wake him or tip his head to the other side. As the train roared through the station George shoved him again, harder this time. The old man's head flopped forward and as it did so, his newspaper ripped from his hands and whirled away in the backdraft of the passing train, the pages separating and expanding in different directions, stories heading upward and outward, some sucked under the train to the wheels, some skidding and settling on the platform as the maelstrom subsided.

George peered at the man, his chin was on his chest and his skin was a shade of grey George had never seen on a person before. Noticing the damp patch in the man's lap George jumped from the bench.

The man remained motionless.

Dead?

Dead.

George looked up and down the platform. No one seemed to have noticed. He heard his train announced on the Tannoy. The surge of adrenalin made him feel better, washing much of his hangover away. Was he the last person the old man had ever seen? George had never seen a dead body before. He couldn't tear his eyes away. His train was approaching. If he didn't get this one, there was no way he'd get to Portsmouth in time to tell Lydia and then get back again to spend the night with Amelia. He stared down at the man, hearing the doors opening behind him, the blank sound of the automated voice warning him to mind the gap, the movement of departing passengers. The man looked like a puppet with the strings cut. His mouth hung open, grey and dark. Dry. The doors behind began to beep. Wondering if he was on CCTV, George jumped into the carriage, just before the doors closed.

Soft Centre

The previous tenants had abandoned some of their stuff when moving out: books in the bathroom, a Japanese doll in the spare room, dirty dishes in the sink. The estate-agent apologised and told us it would be taken care of before we moved in, if we liked it.

In the fridge was a box of chocolates and a pint of separating milk. I opened the chocolate box. Lying on the hard-centres was a piece of paper, folded once. I took a chocolate and opened the note.

> *Sarah,*
> *I love you*
> *ALWAYS!*
> *XXX*

I felt like a thief, reacting with no flash of joy, sad instead, a nothing meant for someone else. I wondered why they'd left in such a hurry. The chocolate was cold and hard.

Sarah had not seen the note but then neither had my girlfriend. I would not make the same mistake.

Jonathan's Shirt

Maria could not decide on a shirt. White seemed the most neutral choice, the least likely to meet with disapproval, but was also most likely to stain, which was why she was there in the first place.

Jonathan sat at a desk in the next cubicle along from Maria. They weren't exactly friends, but they always smiled and said hello. On a few occasions, they'd even chatted over sandwiches.

Maria noticed it almost as soon as she arrived in the office. Jonathan was hunched at his desk and across the back of his shirt were crisscrossed lines of blood. Maria was too shocked to know what to say, even what to think at first.

How on earth had Jonathan got such injuries? Some kinky game? An assault? Self-flagellation? He didn't seem the religious type. He was usually so down to earth. Maria shuddered. It was all so medieval.

All morning Maria wondered what to do. She knew she couldn't speak to him about the marks. She decided to buy him a shirt and put it on his desk when he wasn't looking. Hopefully, he'd take the hint. At present, he didn't even seem to know the stains were there, though Maria had noticed several colleagues glancing and whispering. She glared at them until they dispersed. The morning passed, the stripes, all fifteen of them, darkening to rusty strokes.

Staring at the rows of shirts Maria wondered what collar size he'd be. Her ex had been fifteen, but Jonathan looked bigger. Too tight wouldn't be good but she didn't want to insult by purchasing too large. She opted for seventeen, realising that her dithering had used up almost all that remained of her lunch break.

The queue was five deep at the till, and by the time Maria hurried out of the shop, she was late.

At the junction opposite the office, Maria stepped into the road and was hit by a taxi which knocked her fifteen feet in the air. She landed on the roof of a Volkswagen, bounced off and hit the road where she took a further fifteen seconds to die, doing so with her eyes wide open.

The shirt meanwhile had been catapulted out of her bag and flown through the air to land at the feet of Jonathan who had been sent home early and was standing at the pedestrian crossing, waiting for the light to turn green. With everything else that was going on, he didn't even notice the shirt.

Dear Steven

You must burn this as soon as you finish reading. It would be better for you, if nothing else. Do not read twice. Remember my words and remember my love. My family must never know. What we did was wrong, Steven. I said it and we did it and you told me I was wrong. But it was not right. I have been shown the light. They have told me where I must go and what I must do to wash clean my soul. And so I must. People will say that what I do is wrong. But they are unbelievers. Just as you are, Steven. Turn to the light. It is not too late. There is still time. But time is short. What we did was wrong. It is wrong. You will soon read of me. If all that passed between us means anything, then I beg you, burn this paper. As I shall surely burn.

SCIENCE AND TECHNOLOGY

Electric Lady Love

Milesh had invited me around to his house for a farewell meal. I was leaving London to return to Bristol for a few days before my departure for Japan. Milesh had made it known that he'd bought me a present and was pretty excited about it, as was I; he'd recently landed a major role in a film and was flush for once.

I took the train over and ate with Milesh and his wife, wondering throughout the meal when my present would appear. After pudding, he poured whiskies and looked to his wife who gave an excited nod. He disappeared and when he returned, grinning toothily, he was bearing a gift-wrapped box.

With much anticipation from all in the kitchen I unwrapped the box which turned out to be bright pink and emblazoned with a photo of a semi-naked woman pouting at the camera. Bright blue lettering spelled the legend "Electric Lady Love".

Underneath it said "washable".

Milesh and his wife were laughing, almost bouncing with excitement. I stared at the box in my hands, not even bothering to conceal my mortification.

What were they thinking? Did they think I'd use it? Did they seriously think I'd take it halfway around the world? Even if I'd wanted or needed one, I wouldn't have done that. What if it switched itself on during the journey? What if it was mistaken for a bomb? I could just imagine my case being searched, and the offending item discovered.

"Thank you," I muttered, staring each of them in the eye with slow deliberation, not smiling.

"It's a portable vagina," said Milesh.

"Aren't all vaginas portable?" I replied.

"Open it," they squealed.

Admittedly, my luck with the ladies hadn't been great, but it had never been so bad that I'd stoop to this. Did they think I'd use it or was it a joke? I wasn't sure which was worse.

On the train home I sat at the end of an empty carriage and dismantled the "toy". It was a rubber sleeve fashioned at one end to resemble a vulva. I supposed you'd have to put some Vaseline or something in it. In a little slit at the far end was a metal lozenge about the size of a Kinder Egg connected by wires to a switch. I turned it on. It buzzed and vibrated.

I replaced the vibrator in the rubber vagina and replaced the rubber vagina in the box and the box in its bag and then left it on the seat when I got off at Streatham Hill.

Someone might need it.

Vapour Trail

Michael, his son, sent ear-plugs, but Ephraim refused to wear them; they were made of synthetic material. Ephraim hated everything about the modern world: the bleating telephones, the growling engines, the sharp bite of exhaust – a brutal century's achievements. It wasn't progress, he argued, but regress.

Not that it wasn't his century, just that he was living at the wrong end of it. When he was young, cars had been rare in the village and there were few telephones. The sky hadn't been slashed with wires. Roads could be crossed without the need to look each way.

Ephraim wished to live in the world of his novels – composed with a fountain pen – where clops on cobbles were the only intruding sounds, the sweet smell of horse-apples the only exhaust. He was not alone in his dreams; book sales allowed him to buy a remote cottage in the hills of north Wales. There he could shut the modern world out, far from roads and without sight of telegraph-pole or pylon. Gas and plumbed water were his only concessions to the twentieth century. The peace of an earlier age should have settled on his life.

But the vapour trails remained.

He tried to keep his gaze below the horizon, ignoring the vandalised heavens, those infernal white lines, bisecting the sky.

Still, he heard modernity roar in the air.

Michael's offer of earplugs became increasingly moot as his father grew deafer with age.

If I could go blind, Ephraim wrote back, *I might wheeze on to a hundred.*

Ball Bag Stew

It took NASA three months to verify that the signal was indeed a message and not interstellar scintillation. The communication repeated regularly and was clearly the result of intelligent composition. It took a further four months to isolate which solar system it came from; that of star DB+5deg1669, and shortly after that the planet itself, DB+5deg1669d. Further messages were received, and teams of linguists tried to decode their meaning. It was eventually realised that within the messages lay a Rosetta Stone. With increasing speed, NASA began to understand the messages' content until they deciphered instructions for technology that allowed instantaneous communication across the aeons of space.

The conversation began.

Obvious from the start was the idea that the extra-terrestrials could not be referred to using the current designation; besides being ungainly it lacked poetry. Much thought had gone into how the announcement should be made to the people of Earth and the consequent impact it would have. The international delegation agreed the beings must be named in a way that conveyed dignity, gravitas and lack of threat. While the extra-terrestrials had communicated what was believed to be a term that referred to their planet, their phonology was unknown, as was the etymology; due to lack of shared references much of the communication from deep space remained untranslatable. After much head scratching it was decided that the planet would be referred to as Cerealia – a Roman harvest festival; apt, as a harvest of knowledge was soon to be reaped.

At this point an IT consultant from Fife, Scotland, Dougie Kinnear, stepped forward. Dougie had realised that he'd named the entire solar system seven years earlier on a novelty website.

"I did it for my mate Dave," he told reporters. "He'd found a woman willing to marry him and I thought that needed to be celebrated, you know, celestially! I chose a star system with the same number of planets as there were lads on the stag-do. We went to Benidorm. His lassie was lucky to get him back in one piece! Anyway, I got the whole lot for a hundred and fifty quid. Who'd have thought we'd be writing our names in interstellar history!"

The star itself was named after the stag, Hairy Dave, while DB+5deg1669d was named after a geography teacher from Spalding, Lincolnshire who in his university days had been prone to exhibitionism: Ball Bag Stew.

"NASA want me to sell the names. Apparently, I'm being 'frivolous and selfish'! Seems to me they need to get a sense of humour. If they want to rename our planets, they'll have to come up with the bawbees. They're ours and I've got certificates to prove it."

NASA, who Dougie said could "do one", could find no legal loophole: it seemed the names would have to stand unless Dirty Dougie, who had given his own name to a planet too close to Hairy Dave to sustain life, was prepared to sell the name.

The UN stepped in but even they couldn't come up with an offer high enough to tempt Dougie to sell.

"I bought my mate interplanetary fame," Dougie went on. "I'm no selling that for peanuts. I'm holding out for a fair price."

It soon transpired that despite his generosity in buying the names for his friends, Dougie had retained legal ownership and monetary rights. Ball Bag Stew himself, clearly embarrassed by the whole situation, tried to persuade Dougie to change his mind, but without success.

The gutter press began to refer to the far away beings as "Ballbagolians", "Sons of Stew", or just "Ballbags". Internet traffic on the subject went stratospheric and as it did so, questions began to arrive from what the scientists still insisted on referring to as DB+5deg1669d, or Cerealia. The extra-terrestrials had been monitoring the internet for some time and were particularly perplexed by cat videos, cricket and certain strains of pornography. However, their main preoccupation became the names they found themselves called, their confusion not ameliorated by the sheepish explanations offered by NASA. The communications from deep space grew frosty as they seemed to grasp the import of the Earthling multilogue. While the alien civilisation seemed to lack a sense of humour, it appeared readily able to take offence.

Dirty Dougie remained unswayable. He was now holding out for the island of Grenada, over which he demanded international recognition as President for Life with a million dollar-a-month pension.

On a cold December morning, all interstellar communication ceased.

NASA continued to send apologetic messages, then tried another tack, pretending the faux pas had never occurred, but neither technique produced a response.

Across the world, millions lamented the stupidity of the human race, throwing away contact with an advanced species who could have taught us so much, the greatest moment in history sabotaged by the gutter press. The media tried to reduce the whole thing to a joke, supporting the view held by many that the break in communication was probably a good thing; this was clearly a much more advanced civilisation and Earthbound encounters between advanced and "primitive" civilisations rarely ended well for the "primitive".

Dirty Dougie, sensing that his moment was passing, relented and accepted the UN's bid of $5 million for the planet's name. It was too late, the offer had been withdrawn. No one expected to hear from the extra-terrestrials again.

A month later a new star was spotted in the part of the sky where DB+5deg1669d, previously invisible, was located. After a few days the star had grown noticeably brighter. Not only brighter, astronomers noticed, but closer. It was not long before the Hubble telescope revealed that the star was not a star but a spacecraft. A big spacecraft. With what looked like a weapon on top. Realising time was short, NASA began looking for a way to straighten things out before the Cerealians arrived.

SPIRITUALITY

The Wringer

Yesterday my landlord hung his washing out on the line, shirts trousers, underpants, knickers and a solitary nightie, fluttering like bunting in the sunny breeze.

Three days earlier his wife of forty years had died a slow senseless eight-year death that had sucked her dry and filled her legs with five litres of stagnant fluid. It seemed incredible, five litres, but why would he lie?

I wondered how he'd felt as he sorted her dirty clothes, putting them into colour coded piles according to the cycle, knowing that this was it, their last ever wash together. From now on until the end it would be his things alone, dancing, spinning, coming to rest at the end of the spin, entangled but lonely.

There were none of her dresses, blouses or trousers on the line. For the last six months she had been wasting to nothing, imprisoned inside, propped up on pillows in laced pastel night-wear. Strange for him to have washed her knickers, I thought. For what? Not to hand down or on to the needy. No, just to return them clean and neatly folded to their rightful place. To shut the drawer respectfully.

The Empyrean

After a nasty collision on the M25, Phillip Hockney, an avowed atheist, was pleasantly surprised to find himself in Heaven.

While enjoying Paradise, his pleasure was nevertheless diminished by a niggling doubt: might he merely be experiencing a hallucination, his dying brain unwilling to face extinction?

That he was even having this doubt seemed to confirm the ersatz nature of his Nirvana; was he in fact in a perverse purgatory?

He consoled himself with the thought that, in either case, the experience would come to an end.

It did not.

There There

Words no longer heard. Childhood words. Words of comfort, of someone looking over, looking after. There is no such person now. Nothing. Not lying here. Lying here next to her, her breathing, her rising and falling. Scent of hair spread on pillow. A long inhalation. No one is watching, no one is aware. No one will ever know.

Childish words.

Breathe in. Breathe out. White ceiling. Dog barking. Far away.

And who is aware? Who is aware, waking or sleeping, that I even exist? I, invisible.

I.

Red light blinking, 4am.

All dreams are gone. Ambition surrendered. Football then music, lastly the screen, later the stage. To be pinned on walls, to be seen, to be heard, to exist. To be loved. To settle for this.

It is not enough.

No one is watching. The world spins and space changes. And beyond is the darkness. Do I even exist?

The house creaks. She continues to breathe.

Daylight seems a long way off. No alarm. No cause for alarm. Tomorrow. There is always tomorrow. Always. Always? Always…

I will do it tomorrow.

Breathe in, breathe out. Breath fogs the window. Striving is in vain. What I do is enough. It is enough. Sometimes. To strive for contentment.

It is not enough. It is really not enough.

Red light blinking. 4:02.

Still. There is always the bridge. Tomorrow. I will do it tomorrow.

There they have CCTV.

There.

Heart

Simon was an undergraduate at Oxford studying archaeology, not as bright as you'd expect, as is often the case, but there you go... My friend Jakob warned me that he might start talking about his heart at some point. It was something Simon did after a few drinks, though he'd had tests and doctors had told him there was nothing wrong with him or his heart. He was in his prime, as perfect in fitness as any young man could expect if they ate and drank as he did.

Sure enough, later in the evening when we were pissed, Simon started asking if it was normal that his heart was twinging and asked me to take his pulse. Earlier Jakob had told me to indulge him, but with a few drinks inside the devil took hold. No, I told him, it was almost certainly bad news, a sure sign of impending heart attack. He started crying and it didn't seem so funny anymore. The next morning no one said anything about it.

A few years later Jakob told me what had become of Simon. He'd been on a dig somewhere in Norfolk, it was August, and after a day in the field he and his colleagues had spent the evening in a local pub. The next day he'd excavated and exhumed in blazing heat, sweating out a hangover and wearing no hat. He'd refused food and refused water, working in a shadeless trench, ignoring everyone around him.

In the middle of the afternoon, he collapsed and no one could revive him. By the time the ambulance arrived it was too late, he was dead, a massive cardiac arrest. The coroner said it could have happened to anyone; there was absolutely nothing wrong with his heart.

To the Alps

A fly landed on the skin of Tony's bare arm, ran forward and then stopped, rubbing its legs together as though they were hands. It was iridescent green, the ones that land on dog dirt. Corpse flies. How he'd enjoyed splatting them, ending their buzzing vitality. Doing them a favour, he'd thought, helping them on the karma train. No more crap and corpses.

The fly watched him.

He'd wanted to come here, had told everyone who'd listen, Andrea, his sons, but now he'd do anything to be somewhere else.

He could hear her, her voice low and gentle, somewhere close. No longer nagging, telling him to stop smoking, stop drinking. It'll give you a stroke, a heart attack. Yes, he'd told her, good! He didn't want to end up like her grandmother, a gnarled remnant, plagued by pain and trapped in a body that no longer obeyed. He wanted to be like his grandfather, dead at seventy-five. He'd been found lying at attention having set out on a five-mile walk.

Cheerio! Get out while the going's good…

He'd wanted to come here, had formalised it, written a letter saying this was what he wanted. But now it was actually happening, he realised what a terrible mistake he'd made.

For six months he'd been trying to tell them, to stop their planning. But nothing worked.

He didn't want to go through that door, he didn't want the needle.
The door swung open. A nurse appeared, smiling.
The fly flew. He would be back.

The Sun or the Streetlamp

Something might be happening. Beyond the curtains. Beyond the glass. But I'd rather not know.

She brings me up a cup of tea. I give thanks.

There's a stain in the carpet, hence the saucer.

These walls are getting closer, the wallpaper takes on a life of its own. The lightbulb flickers.

Something happens. I will it.

I'm not sure what it is just yet, but it will shatter glass, blow the walls outward.

It might even tear the curtains.

There is a knock at the door.

Another cup of tea.

I don't bother saying thank you.

SPORT

Home Fans Only

Martin and Janet sat on the wall watching the fans moving towards the stadium, the blue and white of Brighton, the yellow and black of Wolves.

"You can't beat a Gregg's," said Martin.

"Don't talk with your mouthful. You're spitting crumbs all over the place," said Janet, dabbing her lips with a tissue.

"I don't know why we don't do it more often," Martin went on. "Nice to eat outside when it's warm."

A group of young men strutted past, chanting an obscene rhyme, arms wide, cans in the air. Martin shook his head and pulled a sour face.

" 'Cos of your heart, you daft sod," Janet snapped. "They're full of fat, the pastry. And I don't know why we didn't take them down to the front. Sitting on this wall with yobbos going past! You certainly know how to treat a lady!"

"Local colour! Besides, they'd be cold by the time we got down to the promenade."

"Full of fat."

"Little bit of what you fancy."

A passing man kicked Janet's bag.

"Sorry, love."

"Watch where you're going."

Janet slapped Martin's arm and shushed him.

"Never mind, love," she said to the young man. "I shouldn't have left it in the way." She bent and picked it up, placing it on the wall between them.

"Bunch of bloody hooligans. It's like an invading army every fortnight."

"Least they don't scrap much anymore."

Martin snorted. "Beer cans and fag ends all over the place."

A teenager passed, spitting in the gutter.

"There you go," Martin gestured. "Bunch of bloody animals. Needs a bloody slap."

The boy looked back and laughed.

Martin took another bite and chewed furiously.

Janet pulled a piece of paper from her pocket and peered at the writing.

"Just M and S left. Vests for you and socks for me."

He grunted and took the last bite of his pasty, leaving the curve of crust. A group of Wolves fans walked past, taking up the width of the pavement, some in the road, middle-aged, shaven heads. Martin pulled his arm back and launched the crust. It struck one of the men just above the ear.

The man put his hand to his head and turned.

"Martin! What have you done?"

He didn't answer, just sat with his legs apart, leaning forward, palms on thighs, staring straight ahead, a slight smile on his face.

"Was that you, pal?" asked the man, rubbing his head and stepping towards Martin. His friends stopped and turned.

"Eh?" Martin turned to him.

A group of Brighton fans passed.

"He chucked it at your head, mate," said one, pointing at Martin. "Great shot!"

The man nodded at the boy and turned to Martin, taking another step towards him.

"What's your fucking problem, pal?"

Martin smiled. "I've not got a problem. What's yours?"

Janet struggled to her feet and stood in front of Martin.

"It was a seagull," she stammered. "I'm sorry." She pointed upwards. "It dropped it on your head."

Martin leaned around her. "No, it was me!"

The man stared at them, frowning, brushing fragments of pastry from his shoulder. "You're fucking mental, pal."

One of his friends laid a hand on his shoulder. "Come on Baz, let's get a pint."

Baz jabbed a finger at Martin. "You want your fucking head looking at, mate."

They walked off followed by the Brighton fans who had stopped to watch.

"Cheers lads," Martin sneered.

"What were you thinking of?" said Janet turning, hands on her hips. She was red in the face.

He shrugged. "In my day the fans were all mixed."

"What's *that* got to do with anything?"

He brushed his hands together, pastry flakes falling to the pavement. "We should do this more often."

TRANSPORT

Blackberrying

There was a disused railway line near our house that had closed ten years earlier but to me it might as well have been a hundred. My father and I would take walks along the track bed and into the fields beyond, searching for mushrooms that we never found, but my favourite walk was through the tunnel. It ran under the ridge that skirted the western end of the town, emerging on the far side of the A38. At that point the tracks began again, a long siding for trucks serving the quarry.

The land over the tunnel was owned by a man who had made his million after the war, buying up military vehicles and selling them for scrap. He'd kept a few tanks which he parked outside his property. He'd made it known that if the four-minute warning should go, he'd take one and drive into Bristol to bring his family home.

My father and I would walk the cutting that led to the mouth of the tunnel and then into the darkness, the crunch of footsteps on the ballast echoing on the walls. My father would point out the refuges set in the walls for gangers to step into when a train passed. He'd marvel at the efforts of the navvies who built it using only dynamite, picks and bare hands. He'd tell me the story of Henry the Green Engine, bricked up alive. Water dripped from the ceiling, still coated in the black residue of a hundred years of smoke and steam.

The tunnel curved and eventually the light at the end would appear. In the late summer we'd emerge into sunshine and a wall of blackberry brambles from which we'd harvest that evening's crumble. My mother's face would appear, smiling down from the roadside. We'd scramble up the cutting and into our Morris 1100 and then home.

Some years later the man who owned the land blocked up the tunnel and turned it into a bomb shelter for him and his family. Eventually he even filled in the cutting. Now there is no sign of the tunnel. It might never have been there.

TRAVEL

Ergo

We sat outside the restaurant with two beers between us. The moon glowed orange and over the sound of midnight traffic came the chirping pulse of cicadas. Every so often the crossing gates by the JR station clanged and a train would rattle across the broad expanse of roadway. The air was still hot from the roasting of the day, heavy with the odour of baked concrete, sweet with the grilled fish and flesh drifting from bars and restaurants.

We were in clean clothes having showered and changed before coming out, washing off the day and the exertions of love. I was in shirt and shorts, she was wearing a white cotton dress with tiny blue flowers that were just a shade deeper than her eyes. There was a damp patch between her breasts below the sun-blossomed freckles of her cleavage.

We'd been out for hours, talking literature, theatre, film, and music. Now we were onto politics, or rather political theory. I was trying to convince her I was a man worth having.

"Of course," I said, "the trouble with socialism is that it requires a fundamentally ergonomic assumption of humanity's benevolence."

As soon as it was out of my mouth, I cursed myself and hurried on hoping she hadn't noticed, at the same time congratulating myself for not using the term "mankind". It was a wonder my brain could keep up with so many thoughts, I realised, as my mouth raced ahead while the brain struggled to feed it vaguely cohesive words and sentences. The beer wasn't helping.

I thought I'd got away with it but then noticed her frown. I blazed on, hoping to distract her with some other brilliant *bon mot* that would expunge my earlier sciolism.

I'd been rambling for a good thirty seconds when she met my eye and held up a hand.

"Hold on," she said, looking at the table. There was a pause. "What does 'ergonomic' mean?"

I coughed and scrutinised her. She actually wanted to know; she wasn't trying to catch me out. Should I bullshit her?

"Err…"

She looked up and our eyes met across the table. I laughed. I only had one option.

"I don't know." I hung my head, trying to look abashed. "I was trying to sound clever, trying to impress you…"

She stared and I tried to smile, wondering if I'd blown it.

She leaned forward, moving the ashtray out of the way, and put her hand on mine. She smiled and then laughed.

"I thought it wasn't right!"

It was now.

Light from Above

As I slipped from childhood into adolescence, I took to prowling the evening streets of my hometown, usually alone. I liked the autumn and winter best, the cloak of existential gloom, the distant stars, the newfound liberty of nocturnal permission. On the deserted streets the phone-boxes glowed like beacons in the darkness, each one a red TARDIS, shining with potential. I'd never needed to use one, never had anything important enough to say; those who did seemed urbane and glamorous. I longed to need to call someone so badly that it couldn't wait until I got home. Someone other than my mum.

Sometimes I'd open one of the heavy doors and step inside, my breath white in the enclosed space, inhaling the smell of stale cigarette smoke, the faint whiff of urine. Above the shelf with the tatty directory was the list of international codes. I was most interested in the one for the Soviet Union, amazed that I might call there from here, might speak to someone in that far off land. That we wouldn't understand one another didn't matter, just to hear the voice would be enough, like two fingertips almost touching.

One evening I stole some money from my mother's purse, inserted the coins into the scratched slot and dialled the code. The dial spun back slowly each time as I made up the numbers, hearing the clicking in the earpiece, the beating of my heart, waiting for the sound of a phone ringing in a distant room thousands of miles away behind the Iron Curtain. My breath quickened as I waited for the receiver to be lifted, for the voice to speak in a tongue I couldn't comprehend, but never once did my numbers connect, not one combination led me to a voice. Every time just the clicking then the sound of the flatline, high and wobbling, as into the change tray my coins rattled, rejected.

WAR

Naked

Braithwaite, who had been whittling a piece of wood into the shape of a bird, spotted him at sunrise and alerted Corporal Summers. Before long, half the company was taking turns to peer through a firing slit or periscope. They'd all seen men wandering in no man's land, but never like this.

Squinting through the dim light, they tried to identify him, but his face and hair were caked in mud. As he moved across the cratered terrain, the man seemed unaware of his surroundings. His arms hung at his sides and his gait was that of a sleepwalker. Every so often he would stumble or trip. At times he would stop and stare at the ground for a minute, before starting once again, but moving away from the trench to which he'd been headed, and thus he moved from side to side without getting close to either.

Streaked with dirt, his body was thin and muscular, pale against the russet filth of his face and hands.

"Got a fair tackle on him," came a cockney voice. "Got to be British!"

There was laughter and the calls began.

"Over here!"

"Come here, mate."

"Get your head down, you daft bastard. Get over here."

Soon, the whole company was calling, a hollering cacophony, until Sergeant Keele yelled for silence. In the quiet they could hear other voices shouting.

"Kamerad!"

"Herkommen!"

"Komm zurück."

Hearing this, Lieutenant Bowers gave a nod to Keel who got the British lines yelling with renewed vigour.

The man seemed to come to, blinking and looking from one trench line to the other. He stood motionless, arms slightly out from his body. The calling increased in its fervour and the man took a step forward.

He disappeared in a flash and a pillar of smoke.

With the blast still reverberating, silence fell on the trenches.

From no man's land came pattering and thumps as the man returned to earth.

Braithwaite resumed whittling.

The Provenance of the Stories

Some of these stories originally appeared in the following publications:

"Glospak" in *Bending Genres*

"Ergo", "The Butterfly Hook", "Soft Centre" and "Women" in *CaféLit*

"In the First Place", "Ballbag Stew", "The Drunk", "The Last Days of the Edwards Gang" and "The Quarry" in *Everyday Fiction*

"All That I've Done" and "Blackberrying" in *Flash: The International Short-Short Story Magazine*

"A Journey by Train" and "Vapour Trail" in *Fragmented Voices*

"Elsie's Dog" in *Friday Flash Fiction*

"Naked" and "The Pencil Case" in *Ginosko Literary Journal*

"Cul-de-Sac", "Fast Train to Burton" and "Summoning the Toads" in *Literally Stories*

"Mr Happy" in *Obsessed With Pipework*

"Jonathan's Shirt" in *The Odd Magazine*

"Crow" in *Postcard Shorts*

"There There" in *Quail Bell Magazine*

"Her Voice", "Light From Above" and "Nemesis" in *Reflex Fiction*

"Bulldog" and "The Wringer" in *Rising Magazine*

"Donovan's Error" in *Schlock Magazine*

"Dear Steven", "Electric Lady Love", "Mousetrap" and "To the Alps" in *Spillwords*

Like to Read More Work Like This?

Then sign up to our mailing list and download our free collection of short stories, *Magnetism*. Sign up now to receive this free e-book and also to find out about all of our new publications and offers.

Sign up here:
http://eepurl.com/gbpdVz

Please Leave a Review

Reviews are so important to writers. Please take the time to review this book. A couple of lines is fine.

Reviews help the book to become more visible to buyers. Retailers will promote books with multiple reviews.

This in turn helps us to sell more books… And then we can afford to publish more books like this one.

Leaving a review is very easy.

Go to https://amzn.to/4e4Vawa, scroll down the left-hand side of the Amazon page and click on the "Write a customer review" button.

Other Books by Matthew Roy Davey

Into the Water, Into the Flame

Two friends embark on a voyage of adventure only to find themselves trapped in a terrifying nightmare from which neither will emerge unscathed. Joe and Mike are having the time of their lives at the country's number one amusement park, "Terror Hall", but as the day wears on they begin to realise that someone or something is watching them. The boys' sense of unease grows as they uncover the eerie tale of an ancient family whose terrible actions still echo down the centuries. *Into the Water, Into the Flame* is a supernatural tale of suspense and horror.

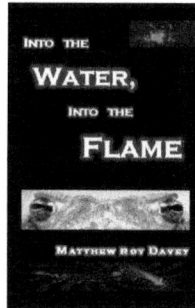

"A great little scary story that perfectly evokes the claustrophobic world of childhood friendships. Ideal school holiday reading." *(Amazon)*

Order from Amazon:

ISBN: 978-1-549555-46-6 (paperback)

Other Voices

Something strange is happening next door, where the houses used to be. It's been a bad year for Alex. His mother died, his father made him move to London, and now he's being bullied. At first he thinks the voices are in his head, but soon he realises the truth is far more sinister.

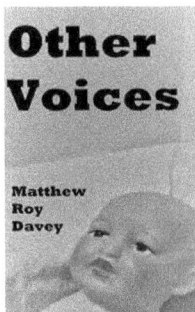

"Beautiful story! I was looking forward having some peaceful time to resume reading the story and get to know what would happen next!" *(Amazon)*

Order from Amazon:

ISBN: 979-8-634294-04-9 (paperback)

Other Publications by Chapeltown Books

From the Beginning to the End
by Henry Lewi

Sure, there are beginnings and ends and there is all the stuff that happens in the middle.

Begin with the Big Bang and end with a distant trumpet call; understand how to send a cheese sandwich into the future, have the origin of the universe explained, and find out how to achieve immortality; and finally add in a splash of espionage. Enjoy the mix.

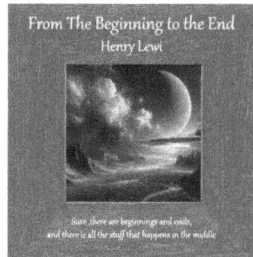

"These stories reveal that Henry Lewi has a terrific imagination and a great sense of fun." *(Amazon)*

Order from Amazon:

ISBN: 978-1-915762-15-3 (paperback)
978-1-915762-16-0 (ebook)

Chapeltown Books

The City of Stories
by Lynn Clement

What goes on behind closed doors? Donna and Jim struggle with an unspeakable act. Millicent encounters something that will change her forever, and Marie dreams of being free from her harrowing life. Melvin's pelvic thrusts have his clients in a sweat, and Sister Francis, the bike-riding nun, has her secret revealed.

The City of Stories is a collection of short, easy-read stories and poems that range from dark tales with a twist, to funny flash fiction that will make you laugh out loud.

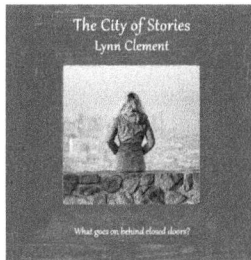

"An art gallery full of vivid word pictures." *(Amazon)*

Order from Amazon:

ISBN: 978-1-910542-81-1 (paperback)
978-1-910542-82-8 (ebook)

Chapeltown Books

www.ingramcontent.com/pod-product-compliance
Ingram Content Group UK Ltd.
Pitfield, Milton Keynes, MK11 3LW, UK
UKHW050844070825
7279UKWH00041B/870

9 781915 762290